I0684211

Cover Design by Unfortunate Designs

Independently Published by Unfortunate Productions LLC

Print ISBN: 979-8-9913742-5-5

NATIONAL VELVET
WRAPPED STEELE

WTF.

UNFORTUNATE
READS

BLURB

After her great-grandmother's historic steeplechase win, every first-born child not only bears her name, but is also responsible for carrying on the traditions of Blue Ribbon Pie stables. Velvet isn't sure training and racing horses is really her calling, until she finds a handsome centaur trapped in the woods.

She nurses him back to health, and Steele can't help but fall in love with the compassionate horsewoman. But to hold onto her farm and home, Velvet must maintain the family's legacy with a win as equally impressive as the one that started it all.

Will Steele help Velvet win one last time? If he doesn't, the woman he loves may lose everything.

This story was originally published in the 15 Shades of Neigh charity anthology.

DEDICATION

I'm sorry to all the horse girls. I've made a grave mistake.

CONTENT CONSIDERATIONS

This is a silly little story about a cocky centaur and a tired horse girl. Some content to be aware of in the following pages includes (but is not limited to) adult language, bondage (in the not fun way), light degradation, half horseman x human schmex, giant horse schl0ngs, horse racing, steeplechasing, familial trauma, injury, mounting blocks of an entirely inappropriate nature, cunnil!ngus, squ!rting, fingering, f!sting, penetrative schmex, unprotected schmex, copious amounts of c-m, a little unplanned exhibitionism, a completely unrealistic portrayal of horse racing in general, and this thing ended up being double the length I planned—so there's an abrupt HEA.

ONE
VELVET BEGAT VELVET
VELVET

"isten, dickhead. If you lunge at me one more goddamn time— fuck"

It was a mistake taking on this horse. If I had just said no, I wouldn't be diving toward the gate of the round pen to escape from a pissed off stallion trying to bite my head off.

You know the saying, 'never look a gift horse in the mouth?' That is some bullshit if I've ever heard it. If a horse is free, there's a reason. You better damn well look in its mouth before taking it on. It could be twenty years old when they said it was five. It could have horrible teeth and you'll have to feed it mash for the rest of its life. Hell, it could be a cribber and you can kiss your pretty barn wood goodbye.

"Not that it would have told me you're a fucking ASSHOLE!" I yell at the flea-bitten grey prancing around like he just won gold at the olympics.

I can't handle any more of this tonight, so I make

sure the gate is locked and that the douche-canoe has water—because I'm not heartless—before grabbing my Yeti and heading back to the house.

The ice cold water feels great when I take a sip, but it would taste even better if it was a margarita. After the day I've had, I deserve one.

Reaching the house, I leave my boots on the porch and push through the screen door into the kitchen. As I pass through, I drop my cup into the already full sink, ignoring the dirty dishes for now. I need a long, hot shower. And I live alone, so the only person I really have to disappoint is myself. Been there, done that. What's one more thing?

My body aches as I climb the stairs, heading straight for my en-suite, discarding dirty clothes along the way. By the time I get to the bathroom and turn the water on, I'm nearly naked.

Once the water is hotter than lava, I step in and sigh in pleasure. All I want is to sit under the spray and disassociate until the shower runs cold, but money is tight and I don't need to be running up my electric bill.

As I run through my shower routine, digging my nails deep into my roots to make sure I get all the dirt and horse hair out, my thoughts wander.

This farm has been in our family for generations. After my great-grandmother famously won the Grand National steeplechase—the first female jockey to do so —horse owners flocked to her from around the world for her expertise. That's how this farm and training facility was born, and why I'm now stuck here.

Starting with great-grandma Velvet's first child, every generation's first born girl has been named after her. Which is why my meemaw's name is Velvet, my mom's name is Velvet, and you guessed it, so is mine.

A weird ass name isn't the only thing that's passed down though, so is this farm and business, whether we want it or not. Meemaw and Mama embraced this life, each becoming champions in their own rites, but I'm not so sure I'm cut out for it. I keep chugging along, though, because part of the stipulations on the deed for this house is that we continue the family legacy until we either win the Grand National steeplechase, or 'sire' a child to pass the place down to. Otherwise, the trust will kick us out and put the entire property up for sale, donating the profits to charity.

Archaic. I know.

Well, my mantle is still void of any gold cups, which means option A hasn't happened. And I'm single as a Pringle, so option B isn't coming around anytime soon. Hence why I'm still here, taking on problem horses and hoping one of them will be the miracle I need.

Nothing productive has come of my water logged self flagellation, so I shut off the tap and hop out of the shower. Quickly drying off and braiding my long hair, it isn't long before I'm snuggled in bed and out like a light.

TWO
BOOM! CENTAUR TIED TO A TREE
STEELE

"How did I get here?" I don't mean that as some sort of existentialist introspection. I mean, I actually do not know how I ended up in the woods, tied to a tree.

Taking stock of my body, I realize it's so much worse than I thought. Scratchy rope binds my front to the tree trunk and my wrists behind my back, and my front *and* back legs are in hobbles. Who the fuck does that?

My chest burns from the rough bark scraping the sensitive skin, and no amount of wiggling is making me any headway. Giving up, I gently rest my cheek against the tree and sigh. The events of the last twenty-four hours slowly creep back into my mind.

The last thing I remember clearly is being given something to courier to Haute Hooves. Centaurs are excellent couriers because we're fast, strong, and human enough to actually talk to people. Horses were great for the Pony Express, but Speedy Steeds is where it's at nowadays.

Squinting my eyes as if that will help jog my memory, a fuzzy scene begins to form in my mind. Ah, fuck. Marauders. I've never had a run-in with them myself, but stories do circulate now and then of centaurs being ambushed and robbed.

I know what you're thinking. *Marauders? What year is it?*

Let me just remind you, I'm essentially a Centaur postman. Roll with it.

Don't worry, it's still the year of our Lady Beyoncé 2025. Unfortunately, some groups of humans aren't as accepting of monsters and "mythical creatures" as others, even though we've been integrated into human society for at least a century now. These idiots dress up like they are headed to an off-brand renaissance festival and trounce around looking for non-humans to bother. At minimum, they are annoying. Then sometimes they are actually dangerous, like in this case. It's like LARPing but for bigots. Not a fan.

Anyway, there was an injured woman along my path, and I stopped to help. We are instinctually chivalrous creatures, some deep seated trait left from hundreds of years ago. Well, I thought she was injured. Turns out she was a decoy. When my focus was on her, something hard whacked me in the head. I can't remember anything after that, but based on the fact I'm tied up here and my parcel pack is gone… yeah I can do the math. Did they really have to bind me like this though? I was already out cold. Assholes.

Suddenly a stick snaps, the sound ringing through the empty forest. I have limited movement, so I'm feeling extra vulnerable not knowing what could be approaching. Is it the marauders again? Do they want something more from me?

A chuff follows a soft whinny before I recognize the familiar sound of hooves crunching through leaves. They are walking at a leisurely pace, their four-beat gait indicating they aren't exactly in a hurry. Movement to my left grabs my attention, and a gorgeous woman riding a palomino rounds the bend in the trail. The mare spooks, stopping suddenly and nearly unseating her rider, who seemed lost in a daydream. I mean, yeah I would probably spook, too, if I were out for a leisurely walk and then suddenly—*boom*! Centaur tied to a tree.

"Whoa, girl, shhh. You're ok." The woman pats the horse's neck soothingly as she coos. "What did you—oh my god." 'Bout time she saw me. It isn't like I'm small. Or hidden. But I'm a little wary, because the last time I saw a pretty woman, I ended up like this. What if it's another trap?

Not wanting to find out, I buck and rear and twist my body the best I can all trussed up like this, trying to get loose before the woman gets too close. It's no use. The only thing I succeed in doing is working up a lather, and potentially spraining a tendon.

"Stay away from me!" I pant out as the woman

approaches. She stops instantly, putting her hands up as if showing me she doesn't have a weapon.

"Hey, hey. I'm not here to hurt you." She says softly.

"Yeah, well, that's what I thought about the last lady I trusted, so forgive me if I'd rather not take the chance." I mutter back.

The woman chuckles and takes a step closer. "Well, it looks like you may not have much of a choice. You've gotten yourself in quite the bind, there. I'm Velvet. What's your name?"

Deciding there really is no other option, I opt to trust Velvet—what a fucking weird name—and tell her truthfully, "Steele." No way I'm telling her my last name yet. One, she'd make fun of me and probably leave me tied to this tree. Two, she doesn't need it to cut me loose.

"Steele." She says my name slowly, like she's testing how it feels on her tongue. "What a unique name." *Says the woman named after fabric.* I manage to bite back my sarcastic response because I really do need her to free me.

When she's just a few steps from me, a beam of sunlight sneaks through the foliage above, highlighting her blonde locks so they shine like the finest gold. Her deep brown eyes radiate kindness, and her body is built for sin. Gentle curves in all the right places, all wrapped up on a petite frame.

"I'm going to get close now, Steele. Please don't kick me." I don't bother telling her I can't because of the damn hobbles. She reaches her tiny hand out, touching my rump to let me know she's there. The slide of her hand along my skin sends a chill down my bare spine, and my cock twitches in its sheath.

She continues talking me through what she's doing in the same soothing voice she was using with her horse earlier. "I'm going to free your wrists first, okay?"

I nod, then ask, "Do you have a knife or something to cut the ropes?"

"Uh, no. It's actually not rope. It's," a ripping sound rends through the air and suddenly my arms are loose, hanging limply by my sides until I can regain feeling in them. She holds up the restraint. "Velcro."

Well, no wonder it was so goddamn scratchy. Her hand never leaves my body as she moves on to undo whatever is tying my chest to the tree. This time the clink of a buckle sounds before a belt drops to the forest floor. My first instinct is to run, but my legs are still hobbled. Velvet has backed up a few paces, likely worried I would turn on her once I was free.

I rub up and down my arms, then stretch them over my head, not missing the way Velvet checks out my abs. I smirk at her, then point at the cuffs. "I promise I won't kick you. Could you undo these, please?"

She approaches, putting a hand on my flank and running it down my leg to the buckles that sit on my pasterns. Soon, the hobbles are pulled away, but I dare not even flinch. I don't want to scare her. She repeats the action to free my front legs, then stands and shows them to me.

"More belts? Are there three thieves running around with their pants falling down now?" I guess it does make more sense than some randos having actual hobbles on them. It's doubtful they set out to specifically intercept me today. She covers her mouth, futilely trying to stop her giggles.

THREE
GOOD GIRL, NICOLE
VELVET

Ha! This centaur is funny! I'm surprised to see he's still making jokes after he was just knocked out, robbed, and tied up in the woods. That thought sobers me, and I stop laughing to ask what the hell happened. "Uh, Steele? How did you end up trussed up like that, anyway?"

He rubs his wrists as he turns to face me. "I was robbed. I'd love to say it's because I was couriering some very valuable items, but the fact that they hobbled me like a *goddamn horse,*" he glances at Nicole, my mare, "no offense—tells me they are likely prejudiced assholes." The palomino chuffs while I feel my face flush with anger. Before I can explode on his behalf, a large hand lands on my arm. "Listen, it is what it is. Thanks for freeing me. I'd like to get back home and just forget all this happened."

Blowing out a breath, I nod. "Yeah. Yeah, okay. I'm

sorry this happened to you. Are you good to get home?"

"Totally fine, don't worry about me." Steele says, but as he turns to trot off, his front leg buckles and he falls to his knees. He tries once more, and is able to get a couple steps before he stumbles again. This time, he stands and hangs his head, muttering into his broad chest. "I guess I'm not fine."

"Hey, you'll never make it home like that. Why don't you, uh…" Am I really about to offer for a strange man—er, centaur— to come home with me to rest until he's healed? One look at Steele's dejected frame, his right fore cocked to keep weight off it, and I know that yes, yes I am. "Why don't you come back to my farm. It isn't far, and you can rest there until you're feeling better. Or until you call someone to pick you up, or whatever."

Steele grimaces when he glances at me over his shoulder. "Normally I wouldn't want to impose, but I really don't think I have that luxury right now. Thank you, Velvet."

I'm a little shocked he agreed so easily, but then logistical questions start taking over my brain. "How are we going to get you to my house if you can't walk?" I ask.

"I can walk a little, and keep minimal pressure on this leg. I don't have my packages anymore to weigh me down, and it isn't like you're gonna try to ride me or anything." He says.

My core clenches when I think about riding Steele in

an entirely different, distinctly inappropriate way. I've hooked up with a couple non-human men, even dated an ogre in college, but I've never been with a centaur. I won't even pretend I didn't check out his eight-pack earlier. He's svelte and strong, but with a boyish flop to his hair that gives him a more laid-back appearance.

Fuck, I'm definitely staring at his abs again. Hoping he didn't catch me, I whip my gaze back to his face. He's standing with his arms crossed and an eyebrow raised at me. Well, so much for that. Steele thankfully doesn't call me out directly, so I turn back to Nicole and pretend like it never happened.

Nicole is my personal horse, and she ground ties like a champ, so she's been chilling here snacking on some tree leaves while I dealt with Steele. Picking up the reins, I gather them at her withers along with a lock of mane, lift my left foot into the stirrup, and haul myself up into the saddle. Walking her up to Steele, I give him a look asking if he's ready, and he dips his head, waving me forward so he can follow.

We keep to a walk for the mile trek back to my property. Even at the slow pace, I can tell Steele is in a lot of pain by the time we exit the woods. The trailhead starts down by the breeze track, I like taking horses out in the woods to cool down sometimes. It's good for them to have a change of scenery, they get bored just like humans do. Just beyond the track is the barn, backed up to several paddocks. The round pen—with the asshole stallion still in it—is just to the left of the large building.

Unfortunately, my house is up a large hill. Even if Steele wasn't injured, it isn't like he could sleep in the guest bedroom. But how do I tactfully ask him where he'd like to stay?

Hey, Steele, I know you aren't technically a horse, but I don't have anywhere I can host you except a spare stall in the barn with my herd.

Yeah, no.

Steele takes matters into his own hands when he calls out to me. "Hey, Velvet? I know this is weird, but is there an open stall in that barn large enough for me? If not I can deal with a paddock, but I'd prefer to stay dry if possible."

Hitting him with a smile I hope is more welcoming than awkward, I answer him. "Yes! Of course, I have a few empty right now. I even have a foaling stall that's huge if you'd like more room. I, uh, am not equipped to host you in the farmhouse at the moment otherwise I would insist you bunk down with me up there. Well, not *with me* with me, but like, in the same house. Obviously different rooms. I didn't mean to imply—"

Steele cuts me off with a low chuckle. "Velvet, it's fine. Breathe, angel. I get it. Just show me to the barn and I'll be good to go."

FOUR
GRANOLA BARS AND RAW POP-TARTS
STEELE

Velvet leads me to the barn, hopping off her mare and quickly unsaddling her. She jogs into the barn to grab a grooming tote, her supple tits bouncing as she runs back out. "Hey, take your time. I know you need to take care of her. I'm not going anywhere."

Velvet gives me a grateful smile, proceeding to brush her mare, currying any sweat away before running a brush over it again. She grabs a hoof pick, then bends at the waist as she slowly slides her hand down each of the horse's legs, gently lifting each hoof to clean it out and inspect it for any rocks. Heat runs through me when I recall her hands sliding down my hind legs, her face inches from my sheath. I was too preoccupied with getting free before, so apparently I missed her tight ass in the air, sculpted by her tight jeans as she worked on me. Goddess bless second chances, I guess. When she's done, I realize I'm nearly panting.

Velvet leads the mare away to turn her out into a paddock, and I use the time to get my shit together. She gives me a beaming smile when she returns before showing me in. When she flips on the aisle lights, I'm a little confused. This barn is huge. It was obviously a show stopper back in the day. But inside, paint is peeling, cobwebs litter the rafters and the bars on the stall doors. Empty stall after empty stall until we get to the other end. Here, five stalls are set up for occupants, the floor spotless and the walls clean and sturdy. A thick layer of shavings covers the floor of each, huge nets filled with quality hay hang on the walls ready for eager equines to munch on it.

The juxtaposition between these stalls and the ones we passed on our way in tells me Velvet may be struggling to keep the lights on in this place. It's clear she takes pride in how she cares for her wards, but if I had to guess, it's just her running this entire operation, and that's an impossible task for anyone. It's not my place to ask though, especially not tonight.

"So this is, uh, our largest stall." Velvet sweeps her arm toward the double stall behind her. "God, I really feel like an asshole offering you a frickin' stall to sleep in."

"Angel." I walk through the open stall-door and turn around to face her. "I'm quite literally half horse. I sleep on the ground most days. This is more than adequate." My eyes drift to the auto-waterer in the corner of the stall.

"Oh, wait!" She exclaims before spinning on her heel and slipping through a door a few feet down the aisle. She's in and out quick, and when she returns she has bottles of water and something packaged in her arms.

"This is all I have down here in the tack room. Sorry it's just granola bars and raw Pop-Tarts, but usually I'm only feeding myself. I could run back to the house and make you a sandwich? Or I could go pick up something? Do you want a pillow? Blanket? Oh or a—"

"Velvet." I cut off her rambling. As adorable as it is, it's unnecessary and I'm exhausted. "I promise you, this is more than enough for tonight. I'm probably just gonna hit the hay as soon as you leave anyway." I wiggle my eyebrows at her. "Pun totally intended."

That gets a laugh out of her and she drops her hands from her hips. "Ok, Steele. If you're sure…"

"I'm sure. Goodnight, Velvet"

"G'night, Steele." She gives a little wave before exiting the barn. I'm not ashamed to say I watch her ass in those tight jeans as she walks away. Centaurs may be known for their chivalry, but I am still a male after all.

FIVE
NO POCKETS
STEELE

"Fuck, you are so tight." I barely manage to force the words from my lips since this slick cunt is squeezing the life out of my cock. I'm unsure who is strapped to the mount beneath me, but I rut into her with long, slow strokes, until her walls are pulsing around my shaft. She is already nearing orgasm, and I want to rip it out of her. Bracing my hooves on either side of her, I thrust my loins faster, unrelenting until she cries out her climax. Her pussy tightens so much I'm nearly forced out, a gush of warm liquid coating my cock and drifting over my sheath.

It's too much, two more strokes and I'm coming, slamming deep into her body as I empty my balls. Never one to be selfish, I pull out of the woman beneath me, the squelching sound of my shaft dragging through the cum leaking from her cunt is obscene. Backing up, I reach for supple hips, gripping them and flipping her swiftly to her back. For a moment, I'm frozen in shock when the eyes of the woman who rescued me last night meet my own. Velvet.

She's heavy lidded and well fucked, but I'm not done with her. Falling to my knees before her, I push her thighs open. Wasting no time, I shove my face between her legs, giving her a long lick from ass to clit, savoring the flavor of our mixed release. She whimpers when I shove my tongue in her used hole, licking up more of our cum. Standing again, I maneuver over her body until I'm near her head.

"Open." Like the good slut she is, Velvet opens her eyes and opens her mouth. I make her wait like that for a moment, before I spit onto her waiting tongue. Instead of swallowing, she waits for my command with our cum on her tongue. "What a good girl. Swallow."

She does as I ask and I move back between her thighs. A throbbing starts in my pastern, but I ignore it, shoving two fingers into her pussy. I rapidly flick my tongue over her clit until she's bucking against me, but her cries seem fainter than they should be. The pain in my leg gets worse until it's distracting. Lifting my head from Velvet's warm cunt, she begins to disappear, her body fading. The rest of the scenery slips away as the ache in my joint takes over my mind.

"No no no no...."

Reluctantly, I open my eyes, not to a sexy, sated woman, but barn wood and shavings accompanied by pulsing pain. I should be ashamed that I was having a wet dream about the poor woman who saved me, but it was too good, and I don't feel any remorse. Actually, the one regret I have is slipping back to reality before I felt her come on my tongue.

Just as I'm lamenting the loss of my fantasy, the sound of boots on concrete echoes down the aisle.

Hurriedly, I roll so I'm laying on my stomach, my legs tucked under me to hide the massive erection I'm sporting. Seconds later, the star of my naughty dream comes into view.

"Steele? Oh! You're up." Velvet exclaims, as if she expected me to sleep in.

Giving her a tight smile, I reply. "Good morning, Velvet. Yes, I am generally an early riser in general, but it was the pain in my pastern that woke me. I haven't examined it yet, but I am betting I pulled something while bucking tied to that tree. Stupid of me, really."

"Oh, god! Shit. Do you want me to look at it?" Her face is full of genuine concern.

"Actually, if you don't mind?" If she wants to touch me again, far be it from me to stop her. With great effort, I haul myself to standing and gingerly put my injured leg out toward her.

She hisses. "I can already tell it's swollen, it's nearly twice the size of your left one. Possible up your cannon bone too." She reaches for me, then stops. "Can I touch you?"

I nod. If she only knew the raunchy thoughts I've been having about her...

Said thoughts are back in full force when she steps close to my chest, then squats down directly in front of me. Her skilled hands start at the top of my leg, sliding down and testing for anything abnormal. Her touch rekindles my arousal as I imagine her on the ground like that underneath me, choking on my cock. It's back in its sheath now, but it won't be for long if I don't rein in my thoughts.

Velvet curbs them for me when she hits my lower leg and squeezes. I let out a grunt as she palpates the area and rotates the joint. She releases her hold and stands, stepping back a bit.

"Okay. I'm no vet… fuck, is that offensive? Doctor? You know what, it doesn't matter. I think it's just a sprain. A very *bad* sprain, but nothing is broken or irreparable. A few days of ice and rest should do the trick." She weaves awkwardly from foot to foot before she asks, "How far away is your home? Can you make it? Or, uh, call someone to pick you up or something?"

I chuckle, gesturing to my body. I don't miss the flare of heat in her eyes as she follows my hands with her gaze. "I don't exactly have somewhere to keep a phone. No pockets." That gets a laugh out of her. "Even if I did, all my supplies and belongings were stolen."

She bites her lip, seemingly having a silent discussion with herself, before giving a cute little nod like she came to a decision. She looks at me. "You could stay here. If you wanted. I mean, obviously you don't have to! But if you needed a place to stay, uh, I have the room. I could even make something up at the house for you. A…nest…or pad…" She trails off awkwardly. Damn, she's cute.

Giving her a smirk, I respond, "I'll stay."

SIX
I BLAME HIS ABS
VELVET

"*A* *nest*, Velvet? He isn't a fucking bird! Jesus fucking Christ." I chastise myself as I head up the hill to the house, aiming to make breakfast for Steele and to find some bedding I can bring down for him. He isn't sure the house is built for someone like him, and I hate to admit he's right. He did, however, assure me that he sleeps on a large mattress on the floor at home, so getting out of the shavings wouldn't be unwelcome.

I blame his abs. There were eight of them for god's sake. Eight tanned, sculpted, totally lickable abdominal muscles. I think it fried my brain.

I made a valiant attempt at staying clinical while examining him, but between his muscles and his vibrant cedar scent, I couldn't help but to sneak a glance at his groin to see what he was packing. His cock was hidden in his sheath, but he did have a heavy sac hanging just behind it. Something about seeing the large, round globes, skin stretched taut along the outside, had me imagining what it would feel like to take his seed. I bet it would be copious. So much it wouldn't all fit in my pussy and would drip out around his cock.

Didn't know I had a breeding kink until this morning, but I guess you learn something new about yourself everyday, right?

My boots land in a pile by the back door and I head directly to the kitchen. I don't have much in the way of groceries here. Cooking for one just isn't appealing, and at six in the morning I'm more than happy with a granola bar and a black coffee. I do have some instant oatmeal around here though, so I dig through my cabinets until I find it. Apples and Cinnamon flavored. I smirk, thinking how appropriate apple flavored oatmeal is for a centaur, then immediately feel like a dick for comparing him to a horse.

Setting the kettle to heat on the stove, I grab two large Ziploc bags and fill them with ice from the freezer. Throwing those and some other snacks in a tote, I wait for the water to come to a boil. When it does, I make two to-go oatmeals and coffees, and head right back to the barn where Steele is waiting.

My core clenches when I walk in and see him stretching, flexing all those delicious muscles. I nearly moan when he grunts, imagining him making that noise while he thrusts into me. How would that even work? Would it fit?

"You're back." Steele's greeting brings me back to reality, blushing when I see the soft smile on his face.

"Yeah, I brought some goodies if you want them," I say, holding out my bounty. He takes the coffee first, letting out a nearly pornographic moan when he takes the first sip. Is anything this centaur does not sexy? It's outrageous at this point. Steele sets the coffee down on the low sill of the stall window, reaching for the oatmeal next.

"Thanks, Velvet. I really appreciate this."

"It's no problem!" I squeak unnaturally. "Let's take a look at this leg, shall we?" I move closer, dropping to a crouch to see if the swelling has gone down at all. It doesn't look like it. Grabbing the ice and some elastic bandaging tape, I fall into a routine I'm used to, setting the ice around the lower leg and securing it in place.

"So, do you run this place alone?" Steele's questions startles me at first, until I realize he must be trying to make smalltalk.

"Yep. Just little ole me with all this room." I reply.

"Why? If you don't mind me asking. This place looks like it could be a major operation."

"It was." When he doesn't pry more, I know he's waiting for me to continue. I haven't talked to someone casually like this in so long, my entire story comes pouring out of my mouth like a fire hydrant. It's like my brain has been waiting for someone, *anyone*, to ask. "My great-grandmother started this farm after winning the Grand National steeplechase. She was the first woman to ever do so."

"Impressive," Steele murmurs.

"Yeah, it was. Everyone thought so, and she ended up becoming a top trainer and jockey. Everyone wanted her to work with them. That's how Blue Ribbon Pie stables was born." I finish wrapping his leg, pushing my hands against my thighs to stand since my joints are stiff from squatting for a long period of time.

Steele looks thoughtfully at me. "And how did you end up in charge of it, all on your own?"

I huff a sarcastic laugh. "This is going to make me sound like an ungrateful louse, but I promise I'm not. I know great-grandma Velvet was just trying to keep both her family and legacy alive."

He interrupts. "Your great-grandmother's name was also Velvet?"

"Sure was." I start tidying the area as I tell Steele the entire story, from the name being passed down, to the requirements I have to meet to keep this farm. His face grows steadily more confused, then incredulous as I go.

"So, she wanted you to be homeless if you didn't win or pop out a little Velvet? That's some Freud level shit if you ask me." He says when I finish.

I shrug. "It is what it is. I've worked my ass off to keep this place afloat, but maybe it's time I let it go. I don't foresee myself conjuring up a champion racehorse anytime soon, and I never really wanted children."

"Anyway!" I straighten my spine and clap to lighten the mood. "Enough about my sob story. I didn't mean to unload all my trauma on you within the first twenty-four hours of meeting you."

He takes my cue, joking back, "Oh, so you usually wait until day two to do that, then?"

I reach out and push him playfully, rolling my eyes, but my heart has never felt lighter.

SEVEN
GOATS ARE CREEPY
STEELE

I can't stop thinking about Velvet's story over the next two weeks. She's been taking care of me day in and day out, even going so far as to find some old cushions to fashion me a bed. All this on top of her other duties, some days coming in just tired, others coming in pissed and sore from yet another difficult training session.

My friends used to give me a hard time about being a perpetual bachelor. I just never felt the need to settle down, especially not with a centauress. There are so few of them born that they have the pick of the litter when it comes to a partner, and I'm just not the type to drop everything for a female, prancing around preening for attention.

I've also never wanted younglings. Not because of any adolescent trauma or anything, my dam was amazing. I've just never had that urge, and I'd feel like a disappointment to any female I mated with.

But on that very first day, Velvet confessed to wanting to remain childless. I never considered there were females out there who felt the same way about young as I did. She's kind, patient, caring...and let's face it, smokin' hot. I'm nearly healed now. Honestly, I could leave now and make it home just fine, but I find myself wanting to spend more time with Velvet.

Of course, she's been the star of all my naughty dreams, too. I've even woken up with a puddle of cum beneath me, like a fucking young stud near a mare in heat for the first time. I'm about to drift off into one of those forbidden fantasies, when the sound of crying reaches my ears. That's odd, I thought I was alone in here. Heaving myself up, I walk toward the sound, only to see Velvet sitting in a stall, her back supported by the wall, clutching a goat and sniffling into its fur.

The goat looks traumatized. Though, those little fuckers always look a little off-kilter anyway with their vertical slitted eyes. A shiver runs through me at that mental image.

Slowly approaching the sad huddle, I knock on the wood of the door so I don't startle Velvet too badly. "Velvet?"

Her head lifts and she immediately lets go of the goat, who runs off to join the rest of the herd outside. She wipes at her eyes as she speaks, forcing faux cheeriness in her voice. "Oh! Steele! I...um...I didn't realize you were awake. Do you need something?"

"Why are you crying?"

She lets out a chuckle filled with mirth. "Straight to

the point, huh?" I stay silent, an open expression on my face as I wait for her to tell me more. She sighs. "The lawyer called today. I've been behind on the bills for a while now, scraping by, hoping I'll somehow end up with a champion steeplechaser so I can keep my farm. Seems my time is up."

She takes a deep breath and slumps her shoulders. "I'm just so fucking tired, Steele."

This selfless woman has been caring for me along-side all her other duties without complaint. She's run herself ragged with a smile on her face. Seeing her on the edge of defeat has me jumping in to return the favor.

"I could race."

You could hear a pin drop in the silence that stretched between us after my insane statement. Then Velvet shakes her head."No, Steele. Even if you were allowed to compete, you're still healing. I won't put you at risk of more injury for a stupid farm."

The more she resists, the stronger my resolve grows. "I want to do this for you, Velvet." She starts to argue but I hold up a hand to stop her. "Centaurs are honorable creatures. I owe you a great debt for saving and caring for me. If I were to return to my village without repaying this debt, I would be cast out." Is that true? Fuck, no. But I'm laying it on thick anyway, and a little fibbing never hurt anybody. I just have to hope she doesn't know anything about mythical creatures.

"What?! That's horrible, Steele! What kind of society

does that?" Her outrage on my behalf is cute. "Plus, only equines are permitted to race."

I smirk. "Well, it just so happens that centaurs are officially classified as equines. Is there a specific rule saying centaurs can't participate?"

Her brows furrow. "Well, no, but—"

"Then it's settled." I reach down to pull her to her feet, holding her and wiping away the last remnants of her tears.

"Chin up, Buttercup. We have a race to win."

EIGHT
THAT'S SPECIEST
VELVET

"You can't race a centaur in the Grand National!"

"Show me the rule that says I can't!" I'm in a standoff with the race official, who, quite frankly, is being a huge dick. I understand it's unconventional, but Steele and I poured over the rule books, even ones dating back to great-grandma Velvet's era. No rule exists stating only certain 'breeds' of equine can compete for the cup.

Steele clears his throat, stepping in to diffuse the situation. "Now, sir. You'd consider the Grand National Steeplechase Association an *inclusive* organization, wouldn't you?" The officials jaw clenches because he already knows where this is going. Steel continues. "You wouldn't want it to get out that you made a speciest decision behind the scenes, now would you? Tsk. Imagine if that made it to the national news…"

The official literally stomps his foot like a child.

"Fine! But you must adhere to all the same rules. No exceptions!"

As the angry steward storms off, Steele and I give each other conspiratorial smiles. "Are we doing this?" I whisper.

"Ready when you are, Velvet." He replies softly.

I don't know what possesses me, but suddenly I'm lurching forward, pressing my lips to the handsome centaurs. He's still beneath me at first, and embarrassment floods me. Fuck. I try to pull away, only to feel a strong arm brace against my back, pulling me into a toned chest. Steele threads his fingers through my hair, pulling my head to an angle that allows him to devour my mouth. And devour it, he does. The way he is stroking his tongue deep in the recesses of my mouth, his grip tightening to near pain in my hair, it's like I'm the only nourishment he needs for the rest of his life. I've *never* been kissed like this.

Steele breaks our connection, panting heavily. "Fuck, Velvet. I've been wanting to do that for weeks." His admission stuns me, but it's the words he says next as he leans into me that leave me speechless. "You couldn't wait until after the race, could you? You fucking minx. How am I supposed to run when I'm half-hard already? You can bet I'll punish you for that later."

With that, Steele scoops me up, depositing me on his back haphazardly, leaving me to scramble for balance as he trots toward the starting gate.

NINE
WE CAN PULL OUT
STEELE

You'd think a big, strong centaur—such as myself—would be embarrassed about being dressed up in fancy colors and being ridden by a *human* in a *horse race*. Annnnd you know what? You'd be kinda right. But I know I can win this thing. Centaurs are, by default, faster than a regular equine, despite what you would assume are aerodynamic disadvantages. Don't ask me how, I failed my *Morphological Comparison of Fantasy Creatures and Non-Magic Species* course in undergrad.

But for Velvet, I'll try my best. If I don't win this race, maybe I can convince her to come back to my little town of Ghostlight Falls. It's in bum-fuck Oregon, but its a mixed-species paranormal town and my neighbors are awesome. I haven't brought it up to Velvet, I can tell it's too soon and she really wants to save her family's farm.

As I trot to the starting gate, some of the other

horses are acting up. Spoiled studs with testosterone-addled minds giving their pony-riders a hell of a time. Internally I roll my eyes, but seeing the horny bastards makes me think about the kiss with Velvet.

It felt like it was out of nowhere. I've been having fantasies about her for weeks, but she's kept herself strictly in the friendzone. In my dreams, I've had her every which way. Ass up on my mounting bench, breasts pushed into the faux leather with each of my powerful thrusts. Kneeling under me, licking my shaft, trying to take me in her mouth but choking on my giant horse cock. I've even invented some pretty creative positions where we could 69 or she could ride me a whole different way.

Fuck, I gotta stop thinking about it or I'm gonna pop a boner. Not only would that be embarrassing, but it would make it a little hard to run as fast as I need to. Could you imagine twenty inches of velvet wrapped steel bouncing around madly as I gallop down the track? I'm liable to give Velvet a black eye.

Luckily, we aren't far from the starting gate. The large, green metal monstrosity looms above, casting ominous shadows on the ground. The stalls we line up in are small as fuck, and they are pretty dark. I just know one of them is gonna slam a damn gate behind me as soon as I walk in, even though I'm not a horse. Honestly, though? I can see why the animals balk at getting in this sucker. It looks like a metal death box and sounds like a jail cell when it shuts.

I walk to slot twelve, staring at the opening and the

rough looking men awaiting me. If one of them tries to man-handle me, I swear to the goddess I'm gonna punch their teeth out. Yeah that's right, fuckers, I have hands up here unlike these other poor, trapped souls.

Why am I so aggressive today? I'm just a courier, not some warrior of olde. It hits me that I'm acting just like these other asshole studs, hopped up on hormones. I look one in the eye as he fights the attendants at the gate. *Yeah, okay buddy, I get it now. Right there with ya, brother.*

"Steele?" Velvet's soft voice brings my focus back to her and the task at hand. Right. Get in the gate. Win the race. Fuck the gir— *no! Bad Steele. Focus!*

"Sorry, Velvet. Got lost in my head there a little. It's a…weird experience."

"I'm sorry, Steele. We can pull out. This has to be so humiliating for you. It's probably unrealistic to think we can win anyway. Maybe fate is telling me to let the farm go." I can hear both the guilt and her sadness in her tone. Instead of answering, I march confidently into the starting gate. "Steele, are you sure?" she asks.

"Velvet, even if we don't have a snowball's chance in hell of winning this damn thing, we won't know unless we try. And I want to try for you." Psh. Look at me being all humble and shit. I'm gonna win, though.

TEN
NOT KINK-SAME
VELVET

Horses to either side of me dance in their shoots, some from nerves and some eager to race. My body is tight against Steele's muscular back. Usually, I'd be crouched low over my horse's neck, but given the centaur has a whole man chest to contend with, I've had to make some adjustments. Luckily, racing saddles are small and light, so it fits on his back just fine. But the bridle was a different issue. I wasn't going to shove a bit in Steele's mouth and hold the reins like he's my pet.

I don't kink shame, but not kink same.

Instead, we rigged up two stirrup leathers so they wrap around his lower abdomen—where a neck rope would fall on a horse if you were riding bridleless—as a sort of grab strap for me to hold onto. I have to ride him, since per the rules equines can't race without a rider, but I don't want to impede him in any way. I'm really just hanging on for the ride.

The clang of the metal gate shutting behind the last horse rings out, interrupting my thoughts, and the next moment, we're off. Steele's powerful back bunches underneath me just before he launches us forward, straight into a gallop. Horses jockey for position as we approach the first hedge, and I find myself smiling. Usually, I'm head down focused on my next move, when to hold back or urge my mount on depending on the course. But I'm not in control here for once, and it's...freeing.

Hooves dig into the dirt, chests heave, mud flings with each stride, and I get to absorb it all in a way I never could before. Never would have been able to had it not been for this unique—albeit extremely weird—situation.

A stride and a half from the hedge, Steel's muscular shoulders flex, his core tightening as he prepares to take us over the bush. I hold the strap tight, then we're flying through the air, horses on either side of us. It's almost slow motion as I take in this experience, because I know we've been in the air less than a second before we're landing on the other side, but it feels like at least 45 seconds of wonder.

We continue along the course in much the same fashion. Steele is an unstoppable powerhouse. He's been in the front of the pack since the start, and something tells me he's holding back. I can feel it vibrating in his aura.

It's the home stretch now. A dark bay stallion pulls ahead. Steele leans forward, his biceps bulging as he pumps his arms. We're neck and...uh...peck? But then, as I predicted, Steele bursts forward in a bout of speed not one of these animals could dream of matching. The pack falls behind as we clear the final hedge, flashbulbs firing as we cross the finish line.

We won. We fucking won! I know I should be over the moon excited because I get to keep my house, my farm. But all I want to do is kiss the living daylights out of the handsome, sweaty centaur between my legs. Fuck, maybe more.

He slows to a trot, then down to a quick walk, looping back toward the winner's circle. I really don't give a flying fuck about that at this moment. Before he can reach the brick oval, I lean forward, stretching up so I can whisper in his ear. "Fuck the cup. Take me somewhere I can show you how *deeply* grateful I am for you. Well, I guess you'll be the one who's *deep*."

I punctuate my plea with a sharp nip to his lobe, and his spine straightens. He reaches back, grabbing my hips to roughly pull me tighter against him. "Hold on, Velvet. You're in for the wildest ride of your life."

ELEVEN
GALLOPING WITH A TWENTY-INCH BONER? NOT IDEAL

STEELE

"Mmph!" Velvet grunts when I slam her up against the wall behind the old racing barn. The paint on the old wood surface is faded and peeling, and cobwebs litter the rafters. This place must have been where the original operation started, abandoned for the more top of the line facility we just left. A forgotten piece of history.

To be honest? I don't give a flying fuck.

When Velvet whispered seductively in my ear, I grabbed her hips to secure her to my back and took off. I galloped away from the track, the press, the photographers. My one track mind was focused on searching for a secluded place I could strip this woman riding me down and fuck her til she couldn't remember her name.

That's how we ended up here. Velvet's legs wrapped around my abs, the heat of her pussy through her thin jodhpurs making me near feral.

"Fuck, Steele! That was incredible," Velvet moans. Is she still thinking about the damn race?

"You're incredible." I tell her. "Shit, I've been dying to have you for weeks. I need to fuck this tight little human pussy. Do you think it can take this massive horse cock?" Gods I hope she's on the same page I am because my dick is so hard it feels like it could snap off. It shot out of my sheath as soon as I felt her hot breath on my skin.

Side note: I was right. Galloping with a twenty-inch boner? Not ideal.

We're devouring each other, lips and teeth clashing as our tongues fight for dominance. Velvet's moans break through each time our mouths separate, both of us gasping for air. Pressing her harder against the wall, I pin her there with my abdomen. My hands leave her hips and immediately grab for her breasts. "These tits. These fucking tits have been tempting me for weeks, Velvet."

She cries out as I roughly massage the supple flesh. She's got her head thrown back, hands braced on the wall for leverage as she desperately drags her cotton-covered cunt over the ridges of my abs. I don't know if my little Taffeta will be able to take my cock today, but I need to taste her and make her come. Several times. And I need it now.

One of my hands leaves her tit to snake between us, cupping her sweet pussy. She moans and grinds harder, and I put pressure on her clit. Even with her jodhs in the way, it must feel good, because she starts chanting gibberish, her head falling to my shoulder as she rides my hand.

"Fuck yeah, Velvet. Take what you need. Come apart for me." Her small teeth find the bare skin of my shoulder and she bites down hard as she climaxes. The jolt of pain nearly has me shooting off without her even touching me, like some young colt.

Freeing my hand, I grip her tight and pull her from the wall. I need to find something to lay her on. I need my mouth on her pussy like, yesterday. There! That old mounting block will do. The abandoned step is made of wood with a large platform on top, anchored to the ground. Perfect.

Trotting over there, Velvet moans with each bounce, her pussy sensitive. A quick sweep of my tail to rid the block of debris, and I'm laying my woman on her back, leaving her legs dangling off the edge. I rip off the offending leg coverings, hearing stitches rip in the process, but I don't give a fuck. "No panties? You're trying to kill me, Velvet," I groan.

Urgency grips me as she spreads her pretty thighs wantonly for me. Laying down, I tuck my legs under myself, lean forward, and dive in.

"Fuck! Steele!" My little jockey tries to shy away at the sudden sensation, but I grip her thighs to hold her in place. Usually, I like to tease my partners until they're trembling and begging, so desperate to come that I know I'm in complete control of their orgasm.

Not this time. I can't wait. Next time, I'll savor her. And there *will* be a next time.

It's love at first lick as I drag my tongue through her sopping wet slit. Velvet's tangy flavor bursts across my tastebuds, making me moan. Flattening my tongue, I lap up every single drop of her slick from her thighs down to her tight little asshole. Fuck, maybe I can take her there someday, too.

"Steele! I...I... Ah!" Velvet's hips cant forward as she nears her climax, as if they're ready to ride my face instead of my back this time. Sliding my hands to grip her ass, I yank her up, lapping and sucking every part of her cunt.

Her legs are nearly spasming now, and the only sounds she makes are a series of unintelligible moans and cries. Reluctantly dropping her back down to the platform, I swiftly slide two fingers deep inside her. There's no resistance as I find the spongy spot on her front wall, tapping and rubbing my fingers against it until I learn what she likes.

Fuck, she's so responsive. I wonder if I could make her squirt. Make her come all over my face. Let her essence drip down my bare chest as I fuck her.

"Velvet, have you ever squirted before?" I ask her outright. Game? Never heard of it.

"Wha...what?" She pants, opening her eyes to try to focus on me. I pull out my fingers, adding a third before pumping back into her.

"Have you ever squirted? Come so fucking hard

you sprayed some lucky bastards face like a Super Soaker? Maybe even blacked out a little bit?"

"Ah! No, I… I don't think… I can… Fuck don't stop doing that, *please*," she begs.

Oh I'm sure she fucking can, she's just been with the wrong partners. Hell, maybe just the wrong species. Centaurs are superior to human men in all ways, clearly. Sliding my free hand up her thigh, I reach her pelvis, just above her mound, and place my palm flat. Velvet squirms, and that won't do. I apply more pressure, not enough to hurt, but enough I can nearly feel my own fingers as they slide past her g-spot.

"Steele! Steelesteelesteelesteele fuck wait! What, oh my god." Hell yes, she's close.

"Give it to me, Velvet. I need it." I nearly growl as I lower my mouth to her clit, sucking on the bud while I slam my fingers deep and upward to meet my hand that's still pressing down. Her walls start to clench, trying to shove my fingers out, a tell tale sign she's gonna give me what I demanded. Never stopping my thrusting, I double my efforts and suck *hard*.

Velvet screams as she comes, sweet liquid gushing from her pink pussy in a powerful spray. I catch what I can in my mouth, not willing to waste a drop. The rest drips down my body just as I imagined. Shifting upward, I push my hand down harder and jackhammer my fingers up and down in her channel with shallow strokes, prolonging her orgasm. I'm rewarded when her ass lifts off the mounting block and more cum gushes from her hot little body.

Just a small movement from my fingers in her cunt make her twitch, so I ease them out gently, and watch as her gaping hole clenches around nothing, begging me to fill it. No matter how badly I want to flip her over and thrust into her, she needs a moment.

"Steele? Holy fuck! Did I just...?" Velvet looks at me, flushed and unkempt, but there's a little trepidation in her gaze.

"Did you just come so hard you squirted all over my face like your pussy was trying to put out a fire? Yes, you sure as fuck did, my little fire hydrant." I want to let her come down from her high slowly, but my rock hard cock is weeping, crying tears of precum in its desperation to sink deep into Velvet's warm body.

Leaning down, I kiss my way up her body, pushing her top up as I go. Once her shirt is just above her breasts, the sight of her tightly bound tits makes me want to free them. Slipping my fingers under her sports bra, I shove it up just enough to expose her ivory globes. I don't have the patience to get her naked, but I do pause to wrap my lips around each mauve nipple. I'll have to give them more attention later. Popping the second taut bead from my mouth, I drag my tongue toward her ear, following the motion with my hand, sliding until my fingers wrap around her pretty throat to tip her head up, forcing her to look at me.

"There she is," I mutter. "Are you ready, Velvet? To take my giant cock? I need to fuck you, please say I can." I'm not above begging at this point. She tries to nod, but my fingers keep her head in place. "Say it out loud, Velvet. *Can I fuck you*?"

"Yes. Yes yes yes, please fuck me, stud." She smirks. Oooh, so my sweet girl wants to be a brat now? I guess I just have to fuck that right out of her.

TWELVE
A FEW MORE INCHES?!
VELVET

Steele's predatory glare is the only warning I get that I may have fucked up. I don't know what made me taunt him—I'm blaming the brain cells that probably flew out of my body with the copious amounts of cum. Seriously, Steele's chest still glistens with my release. It's kinda hot.

My centaur's lips tip into a smug grin, then his large hands are on my hips, gripping me with enough force to leave bruises. "Ooooh!" I cry out as I'm hauled bodily upward and flipped onto my stomach. The rough surface of the aged wood beneath me sends tingles through my body when they rub against my over-sensitive skin. Steele positions me on my hands and knees, ass in the air. One large hand leaves my hip to slide up my spine, pushing my torso down until my cheek hits the wood.

"Don't. Move." Steele's voice sounds feral. Like I'd

move now when he's about to stuff me full of centaur cock. I've wanted this for weeks.

He spreads my knees further apart, then pulls my ass cheeks apart. The cool air hits my pussy and makes me shiver. "Are you sure you can take me, Velvet?" Steele asks.

To be honest, I'm not sure I can. Regardless, I nod as best I can while keeping my face to the platform. "I don't know, that cunt was almost too tight for three of my fingers. I think I need to stretch you out a little more, hmm?"

Three fingers slam into me from behind with no warning. *Fuck.* When my body opens to him, he adds another finger, and I'm not sure I've ever felt so deliciously full. But I know damn well that even four of Steele's thick digits doesn't compare to his thick horse cock.

"That's it. Good girl. Can you take more?" he coos. More? What more can he give me if it isn't his dick. His fingers slide nearly all the way out, and I whimper at the loss until I feel him pushing at my entrance again, this time even thicker than before. *Oh. Oh my god.*

"If you can take my whole fist, you can take my cock. Are you gonna relax and open for me? Let me in?" Steele confirms my suspicions when he breaches my entrance, twisting his hand back and forth to wiggle into my body. His knuckles hit my entrance, and my pussy resists for a moment until he pushes more, and they pop inside. Now that the widest part of his fist is past the rim, my channel greedily sucks the rest of his hand in like a hoover, pulsing desperately around it.

"Fuck, Velvet. You're taking my whole godsdamned fist. That's a good fucking girl. Take it all," he praises as he leans over my back, resting his elbow on the wood next to my body, He's so fucking deep, and I'm so fucking close. Steele continues punching my pussy like a champion boxer, then pinches my nipple and tweaks it hard. The bite of pain does it, and I go flying over the cliff again.

He's still got a death grip on my breast when he yanks his arm from my body, then that, too, is gone. Steele's shadow looms over me as he rears up to place his hooves on either side of me. Holy shit, he's going to rut me like an animal. What's even more surprising, is I want him to.

A long, hard, shaft slides up my inner thigh, poking around at the apex until the head of his cock notches at my entrance. We both groan as he pushes the tip inside, then rocks back and forth until he can get deeper, and deeper, and deeper. Just as I begin to feel too full, Steele stops.

"You're doing so good, Velvet. Only a few more inches to go." He tries to reassure me.

A few more inches?! He's gonna impale a lung if he goes any deeper. I don't want him to stop, though, so arch my back, angling my hips to take more, silently urging him on. He takes the hint and pushes forward, forcing the rest of his humongous cock into my pussy.

When his large body covers mine completely, a shot

of fear hits me momentarily. I've been kicked, bitten, and trampled by horses in the past. It makes sense my body would respond instinctively. But at the same time, my core tightens around Steele's shaft, making him groan. Well, I'm learning a lot about myself.

1. I'm attracted to centaurs.
2. I can squirt a whole ass river with the right partner.
3. My pussy can take so much more dick than I ever imagined.
4. A little fear turns me on. Apparently.

"*Fuck*! You're a dirty little cent-whore, aren't you? No human dick will ever be good enough for you again. Ah! Fuck yes! Milk my cock with your slutty little pussy, Velvet."

Oh.

5. I like degradation.

Steele's thrusts are so hard, it's all I can do just to hold onto the mounting block lest I go flying forward with each snap of his powerful hips. He can't hold my ass up when he's buried inside me, so I'm using all my core strength to push back against him, meeting his strokes.

I'm so close. But can I really come three times in a row? Seems a little greedy, but I'm not gonna fight it, that's for sure. I want to touch my clit, but I can't let go of the wood. Or can I?

Fuck it.

Releasing my death grip on the planks, I let my upper body hold my weight. The rough surface of the pine bites at my nipples as they drag across it, heightening my arousal. One hand shoves its way between my thighs, finding the throbbing bud unerringly. I start circling it, sliding across it, anything until I feel that telltale tension build in my core. The familiar tingle of heat crawling up my spine. The new angle from my altered positioning ensures Steele's cock hits even deeper, the ridge under the head sliding over my g spot every time. Desperate. I shove my other hand under me, using it to spread my lips so I can have direct access to my clit. I pinch the nub and that does it. I'm crossing the finish line once more, screaming out Steele's name in my ecstasy.

"Gods, yes. Come on this cock. Soak my fucking balls, Velvet." Steele's hooves shift on either side of me. The left one paws at the surface I'm lying on. I can hear his long tail twitching madly. "I'm gonna...ooohhh fuuckkkkkk!" Steele gives one last shaky thrust, then he's filling me with his hot load. It already drips out of me and he hasn't even finished yet. I suppose it has nowhere else to go but out with Steele's mega-cock rearranging my insides.

A couple tiny jerks of his hips later, Steele stays buried inside me, breathing heavily. He pulls out, and more cum leaks from my battered hole. Fuck, I don't think I wanna look at that later.

Once he's finally free, he carefully backs down off the block, falling to his knees behind me. Strong hands rub up and down my back, my thighs, everywhere he can reach, but all I can do is lay here like a limp noodle. A satisfied limp noodle, but a noodle nonetheless.

Until Steele gently pulls me to stand, turning me around before helping me sit back on the mounting block before him. In complete juxtaposition to the rutting beast he was moments ago, my centaur slowly spreads my thighs, kissing the inside of each knee. Then he shocks the hell out of me by dragging his tongue up my thighs, through his own cum. He descends on my pussy again, but this time its not frenzied. It's slow, gentle, almost soothing as he laps up our combined release. Leaning back on one hand, I run my fingers through Steele's hair with the other, totally content to let this hot centaur take his time cleaning me up.

THIRTEEN
MY SWEET LITTLE JOCKEY
STEELE

The taste of my cum mixed with Velvet's release may just be my new addiction. I can't believe I lost control like that. More importantly, I can't believe my sweet little jockey took it all like a champ.

When I've had my fill, I nuzzle her perfect cunt before rising to my full height. She's splayed out before me, her body flushed red from a good fucking, her clothes only half removed. My heart tightens, and I lean down to help right her bra and top, looking around for the jodhpurs I flung somewhere in my haze.

Ah ha! There they are, a pile of crumpled tan fabric peeks out from under the mounting block. I help her into them, but nothing can hide that just-been-fucked glow she's sporting.

"You okay?" I ask when I realize we've been moving in silence this whole time. I'm afraid she's regretting her choice now. Since when did I become an insecure asshole? But when Velvet answers, she looks me straight in the eye, unashamed of our tryst. *That's my girl.*

She smiles. "I'm better than okay, Steele. Were you not paying attention? I came three times, once so hard I nearly blacked out." She chuckles and takes my hand. "Though I can't believe we just did that out in the open. Where are we anyway?" she asks as she looks around.

"Honestly? I have no fucking clue. Some old training facility maybe? Didn't care at the time. Still don't, actually." I'd have fucked her in the winner's circle if she'd have let me. But something tells me neither Velvet or the race officials would like that.

"I guess we should get back down there, huh?" She looks out over the fields, squinting as the setting sun hits her directly in the eyes.

"Well, you did win. You should probably go handle all that." I reply.

"Me? Oh no. *We* won and *we* will be handling 'all that.' Together."

Yeah, together. I like the sound of that.

ABOUT THE AUTHOR

Cassie is an ADHD millennial mom of one from Baltimore who loves craft beer and chaos. Though she runs the Unfortunate Reads page, she reads and enjoys more than just the absolutely unhinged stories. She likes her books extra spicy, with a special fondness for PNR, Sci/fi, and Why Choose romance.

She began publishing in 2024, and quickly caught the writing bug. She is also a narrator, cover designer, and generally can't pick one facet of the book world to stay in.

unfortunatereads.com

ALSO BY AUTHOR

By Unfortunate Reads

Handle Me

Pushin' Cushions

(co-write with Vera Valentine)

Fully Charged

(co-write with Nicole Parker)

Santa's Sack

(co-write with Nicole Parker)

Sentient Object Holiday Shared Series

My Date With Water

My Date With a Jellyfish

———

By Clover Holloway

Zero to 69

(co-write with Thea Masen and Kate McDarris)

Welcome to Bone Town

(co-write with Thea Masen)

Slip into Me

**UNCENSORED VERSON
ON PATEREON**